D0422589

WITHDRAWN

Y793.73 MARZOLLO
Marzollo, Jean.
I spy an egg in a nest / rid
M 371648 02/24/11
New Albany-Floyd Co. Library

NAFC PUBLIC LIBRARY

I SPY

AN EGG IN A NEST

For Owen, Kei, Grace, and Will,
with thanks to Dan and Dave
—J.M.

For Agnes Sallick
—W.W.

No part of this publication may be reproduced, stored in a retrieval system, or transmitted in any form or by any means, electronic, mechanical, photocopying, recording, or otherwise, without written permission of the publisher. For information regarding permission, write to Scholastic Inc., Attention: Permissions Department, 557 Broadway, New York, NY 10012.

Text copyright © 2011 by Jean Marzollo.
Cover illustration (and first spread) "Nature" from *I Spy: a Book of Picture Riddles* © 1992 by Walter Wick; "Into the Woods" from *I Spy Fantasy* © 1994 by Walter Wick; "Prizes to Win" from *I Spy Fun House* © 1993 by Walter Wick; "Clouds" from *I Spy Fantasy* © 1994 by Walter Wick; "The Golden Cage" from *I Spy Mystery* © 1993 by Walter Wick; "The Rainbow Express" from *I Spy Fantasy* © 1994 by Walter Wick; "Puppet Theater" from *I Spy Fun House* © 1993 by Walter Wick; "Silhouettes" from *I Spy: A Book of Picture Riddles* © 1992 by Walter Wick; "View from the Fort" from *I Spy Treasure Hunt* © 1999 by Walter Wick; "Toys in the Attic" from *I Spy: A Book of Picture Riddles* © 1992 by Walter Wick.

All rights reserved. Published by Scholastic Inc.
SCHOLASTIC, CARTWHEEL BOOKS, and associated logos
are trademarks and/or registered trademarks of Scholastic Inc.
Lexile is a registered trademark of MetaMetrics, Inc.

Library of Congress Cataloging-in-Publication Data
Marzollo, Jean.
I spy an egg in a nest / by Jean Marzollo ; photographs by Walter Wick.
p. cm. -- (Scholastic reader. Level 1)
ISBN 978-0-545-22093-4
1. Picture puzzles--Juvenile literature. I. Wick, Walter, ill. II. Title. III. Series.
GV1507.P47M2924 2011
793.73--dc22 2009051611

ISBN 978-0-545-22093-4

10 9 8 7 6 5 4 3 2 1 11 12 13 14 15

Printed in the U.S.A. 40 • First printing, January 2011

I SPY

AN EGG IN A NEST

Riddles by Jean Marzollo
Photographs by Walter Wick

SCHOLASTIC INC.
New York Toronto London Auckland
Sydney Mexico City New Delhi Hong Kong

I spy

a butterfly,

two small stones,

an egg in a nest,

and two pinecones.

I spy

a tire, 

antlers,

a skunk, 

and a woman who lives
inside a tree trunk.

I spy

a flamingo,

a red bull's-eye,

a yellow umbrella,

and a blue bow tie.

I spy

a flag,

an angel's wing,

a unicorn's horn,

a hat,

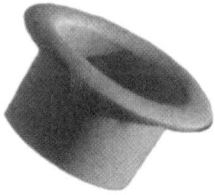

and a string.

I spy

a cactus,

a tiny door,

a painted flower,

and a real one on the floor.

I spy

a craft stick,

a cave's yellow glow,

two paintbrushes,

and a pretty rainbow.

I spy

a cane,

a lamb,

a red ball,

a W block,

and a dog that's small.

I spy

a fireman,

a gear,

a dragon,

a baseball player's glove,

and a little toy wagon.

I spy

a picnic table, 

 a little tan dog,

a man with blue yarn, 

 and a peaceful frog.

CHARLY'S
CLAMS

I spy

a basket,

a 6 by a 3,

a really strong man,

and a block with a G.

Past
Mr. ATHEL ETIC CRANK
Miss NOVELRI
OLD MAID'S CAT
GAME OF
STORE
PLAY CUCKOO FOR FUN.
F
G

I spy two matching words.

yellow umbrella

cave's yellow glow

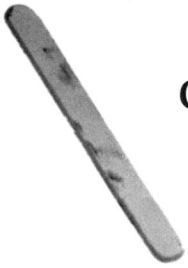

craft stick

I spy two matching words.

man with blue yarn

hat

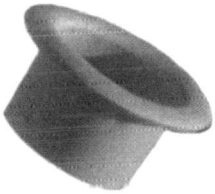

really strong man

I spy two words that start with the letter C.

lamb

cane

cactus

I spy two words that start with the letters FL.

flamingo

fireman

flag

I spy two words that end with the letter T.

butterfly 

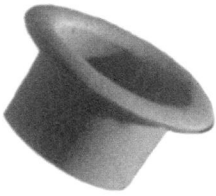 hat

basket 

I spy two words that end with the letters ER.

baseball player

painted flower

unicorn's horn

I spy two words that rhyme.

butterfly 

 dog that's small

blue bow tie 

I spy two rhymes.

6 by a 3

block with a G

red bull's-eye